HELLO MUD[DUH] HELLO FADDAH!
(A LETTER FROM CAMP)

by **Allan Sherman** and **Lou Busch**
illustrated by **Jack E. Davis**

SCHOLASTIC INC.
New York Toronto London Auckland Sydney
Mexico City New Delhi Hong Kong Buenos Aires

For Lucy, Janey, and Vincent
J.E.D.

ISBN-13: 978-0-545-01821-0
ISBN-10: 0-545-01821-8

Words by Allan Sherman. Music by Lou Busch. Copyright © 1963 (Renewed 1991) by WB Music Corp. and Burning Bush Music. Lyrics reprinted by permission of Warner Bros. Publications. Illustrations copyright © 2004 by Jack E. Davis. All rights reserved. Published by Scholastic Inc., 557 Broadway, New York, NY 10012, by arrangement with Dutton Children's Books, a division of Penguin Young Readers Group, a member of Penguin Group (USA) Inc. SCHOLASTIC and associated logos are trademarks and/or registered trademarks of Scholastic Inc.

12 11 10 9 8 7 6 5 4 3 2 1   7 8 9 10 11 12/0

Printed in the U.S.A.   40

First Scholastic printing, June 2007

Designed by Richard Amari

Camp is very entertaining,

and they say we'll have some
fun if it stops raining.

I went hiking with Joe Spivy.

He developed poison ivy.

He got ptomaine poisoning last night after dinner.

All the counselors
hate the waiters,

and the lake has alligators,

Take me home, I promise
I will not make noise
or mess the house with other boys.

Let me come home if you miss me.
I would even let Aunt Bertha hug and
kiss me.

Muddah, Faddah, kindly disregard this letter.